AN EARTH-BOT'S SOLUTION TO
PLASTIC POLLUTION

This book is dedicated to Oceana.org

Published in Canada and the U.S. by Kids Can Press Ltd.
25 Dockside Drive, Toronto, ON M5A 0B5

Kids Can Press is a Corus Entertainment Inc. company

www.kidscanpress.com

The artwork in this book was rendered in pencil and digitally.
The text is set in Absent Grotesque Light.

Edited by Yasemin Uçar
Designed by Michael Reis

Printed and bound in Heyuan, China, in 3/2021 by Asia Pacific Offset

CM 21 0 9 8 7 6 5 4 3 2 1

Library and Archives Canada Cataloguing in Publication

Title: An earth-bot's solution to plastic pollution / Russell Ayto.
Names: Ayto, Russell, author, illustrator.
Identifiers: Canadiana 20200231464 | ISBN 9781525305382 (hardcover)
Classification: LCC PZ7.1.A98 Ea 2021 | DDC j823/.92 — dc23

Kids Can Press gratefully acknowledges that the land on which our office is located is the traditional territory of many nations, including the Mississaugas of the Credit, the Anishnabeg, the Chippewa, the Haudenosaunee and the Wendat peoples, and is now home to many diverse First Nations, Inuit and Métis peoples.

We thank the Government of Ontario, through Ontario Creates; the Ontario Arts Council; the Canada Council for the Arts; and the Government of Canada for supporting our publishing activity.

FSC
www.fsc.org
MIX
Paper from responsible sources
FSC® C012521

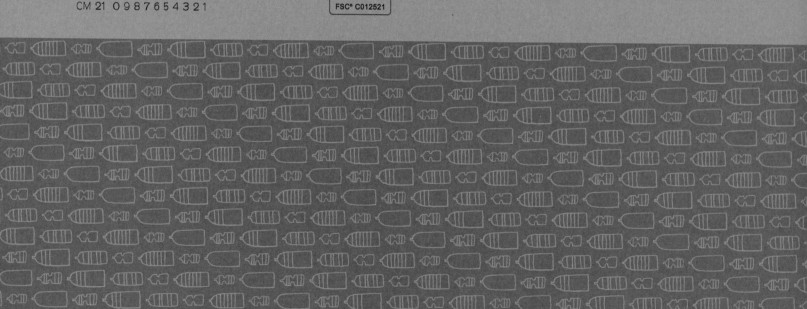

AN EARTH-BOT'S SOLUTION TO
PLASTIC POLLUTION

RUSSELL AYTO

KIDS CAN PRESS

Neo lives next to the ocean.
    The ocean has a big problem — it's called
plastic pollution.

Plastic pollution is also a big problem in Neo's room.

His room is a complete mess. Grandpa calls it "an area of outstanding danger to nature."

But Neo doesn't notice.
He is too busy playing
video games.

Neo's favorite game is Space Cabbages. It mostly involves defending the planet Earth against invading aliens by chucking cabbages at them.

But Neo can never save the planet on his own. There are too many aliens. He can only win if all the Earth-Bots join in and help chuck loads more cabbages.

Grandpa thinks Neo should be mostly defending his room against all the invading trash instead.

Today, Grandpa is popping out to a reunion party for astronauts. He is also hoping for a miracle — in Neo's room.

Before leaving, he shows Neo a feather duster, a vacuum cleaner and a recycling bin.

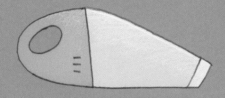

But Neo is busy playing
Space Cabbages.

"You use them to clean up
a room," he says. "And don't
forget to put the recycling
out. Toodle pip."

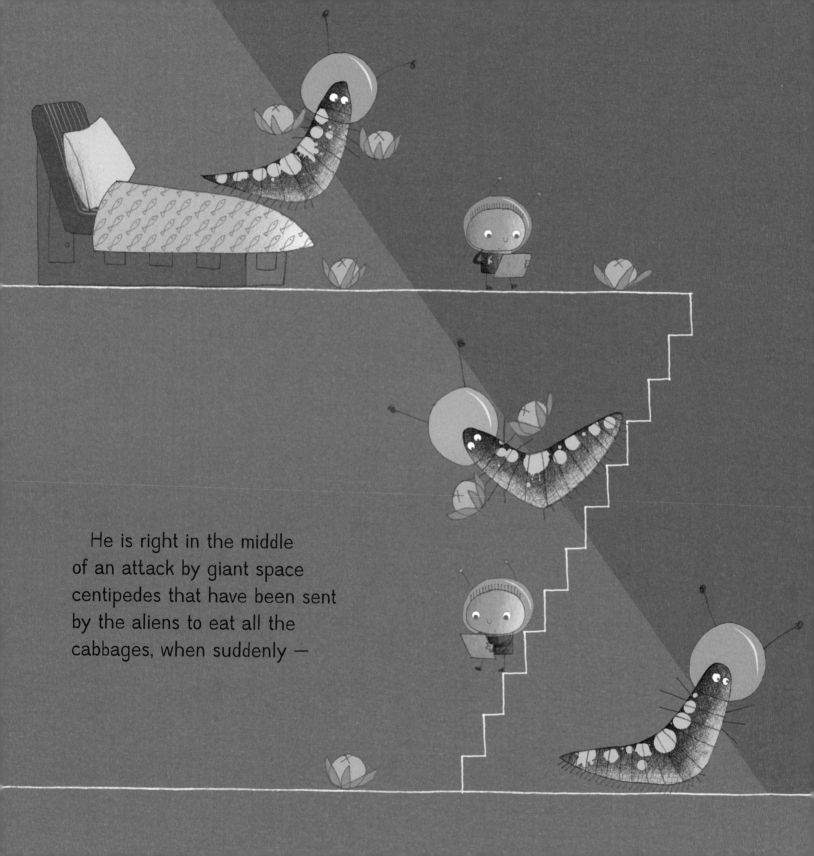

He is right in the middle of an attack by giant space centipedes that have been sent by the aliens to eat all the cabbages, when suddenly —

Tap. Tap. Tap.

Somebody knocks at the door.
Neo is hoping it is not an alien.

It's a seal.
"Please can you help us? Plastic pollution is ruining our ocean and we need to clean it up."

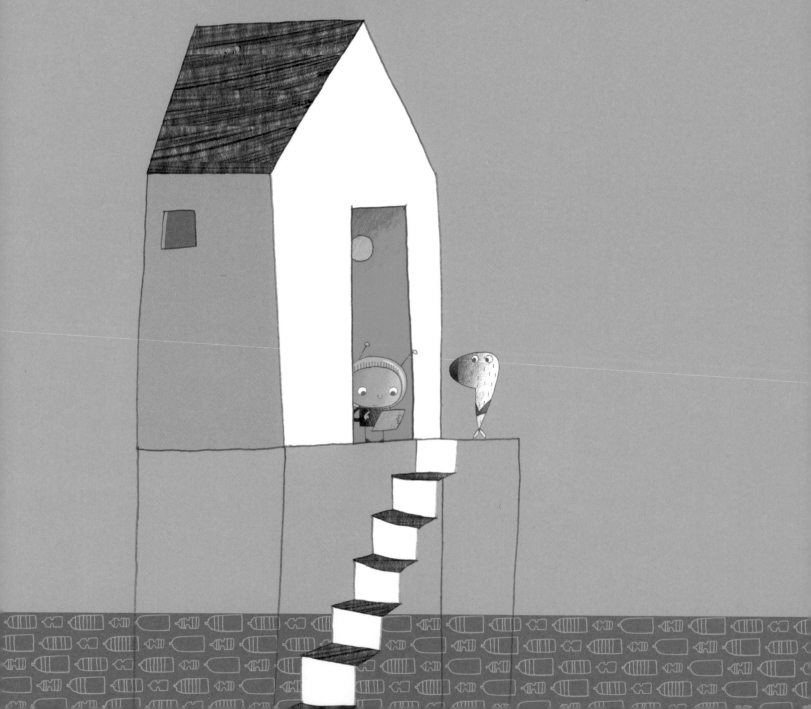

"Sorry, I'm busy saving the planet," says Neo.
"But here's a feather duster. Grandpa says you
use it to clean up a room. Goodbye."
And Neo goes straight back to
chucking cabbages.

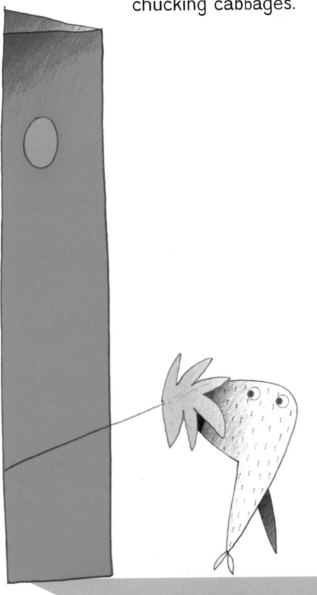

Tap. Tap. Tap.

This time, it's a penguin and a turtle.

"Please can you help us? Plastic pollution is ruining our ocean and we need to clean it up."

"Sorry. I'm too busy," says Neo.
"Have a vacuum cleaner and a
recycling bin. Goodbye."

But the ocean isn't dusty. The trash keeps floating away ...

AND THAT FISH IS **NOT** MADE OF PLASTIC!

Tap. Tap. Tap ...

TAP. TAP. TAP ...

TAP. TAP. TAP ...

"NOW WHAT?"

"None of these things work underwater," says the seal. "And we really need to clean up our ocean. Come and look."

"All right. If you promise to stop interrupting my Space Cabbages."

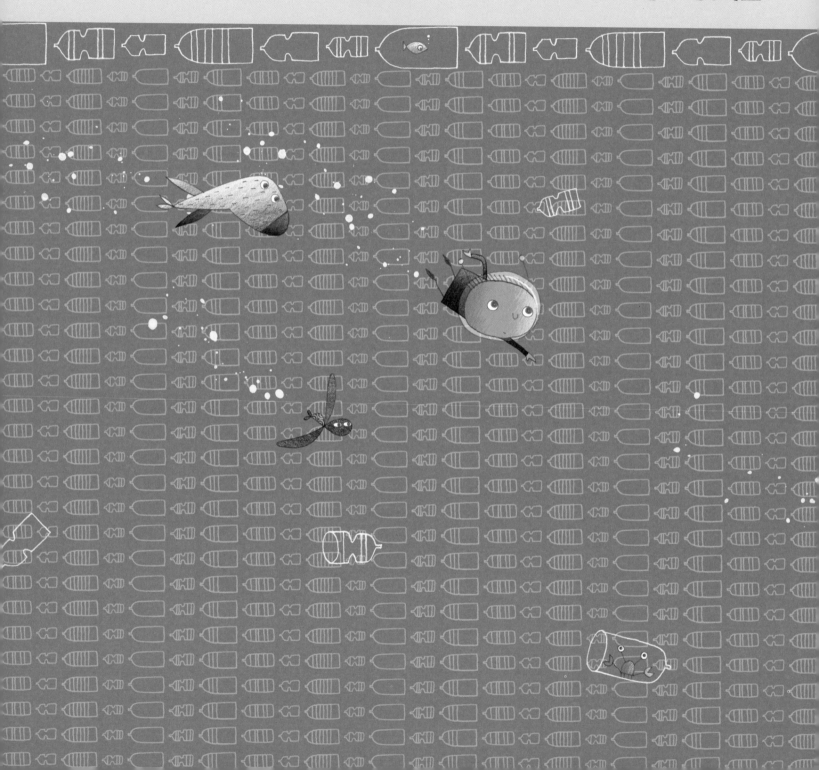

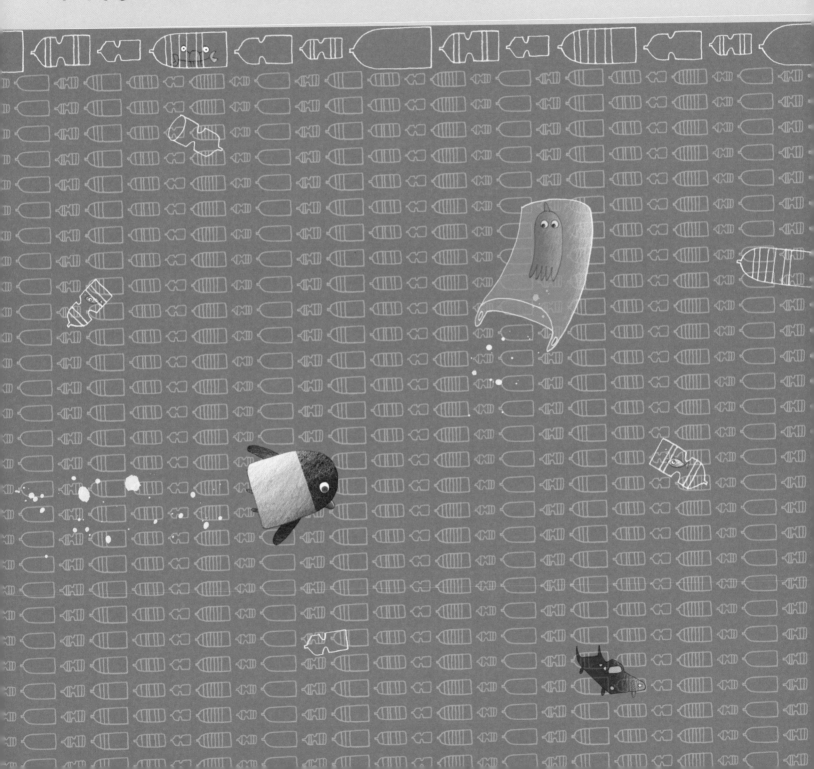

PROPER CATASTROPHE!"

Neo can't believe what's in front of his face.
"How on Earth did your ocean get into a
bigger mess than my room?"

"People are using too much plastic!"
says the seal.
"Watch out! Here comes
Mr. Humpback!" says the penguin.

"Look!" says the turtle. "He's
swallowing all that plastic by
accident ..."

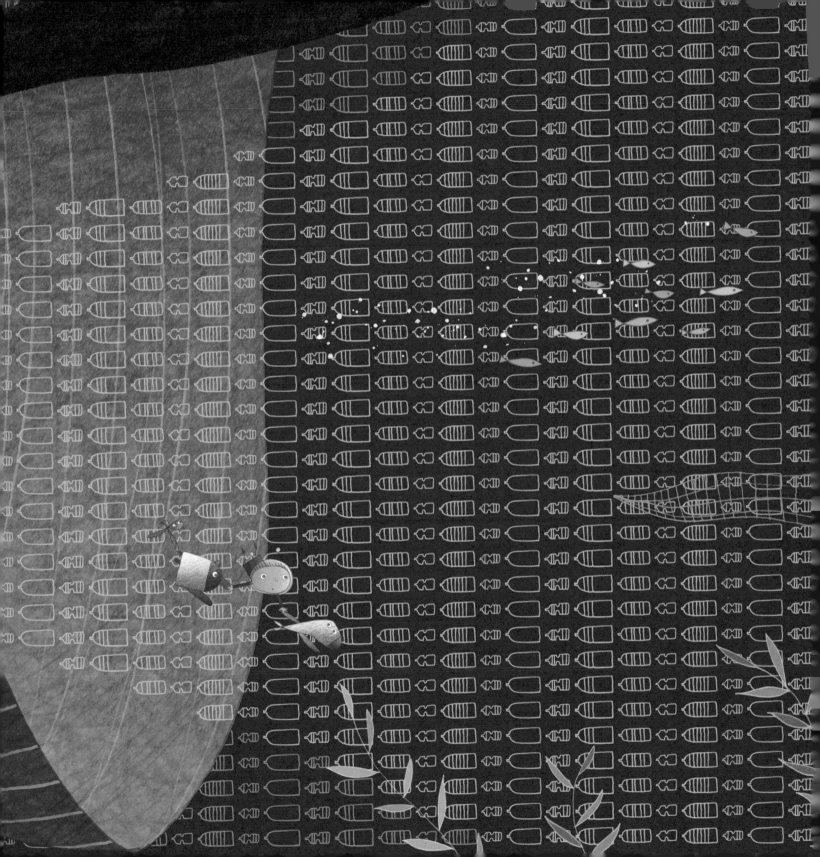

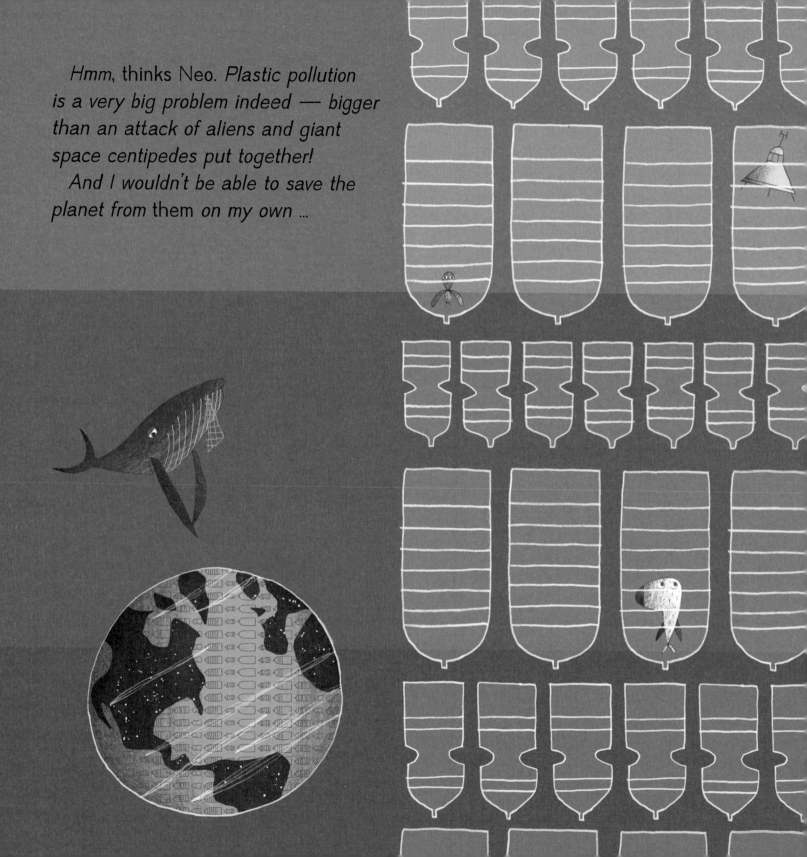

Hmm, thinks Neo. *Plastic pollution is a very big problem indeed — bigger than an attack of aliens and giant space centipedes put together!*

And I wouldn't be able to save the planet from them on my own ...

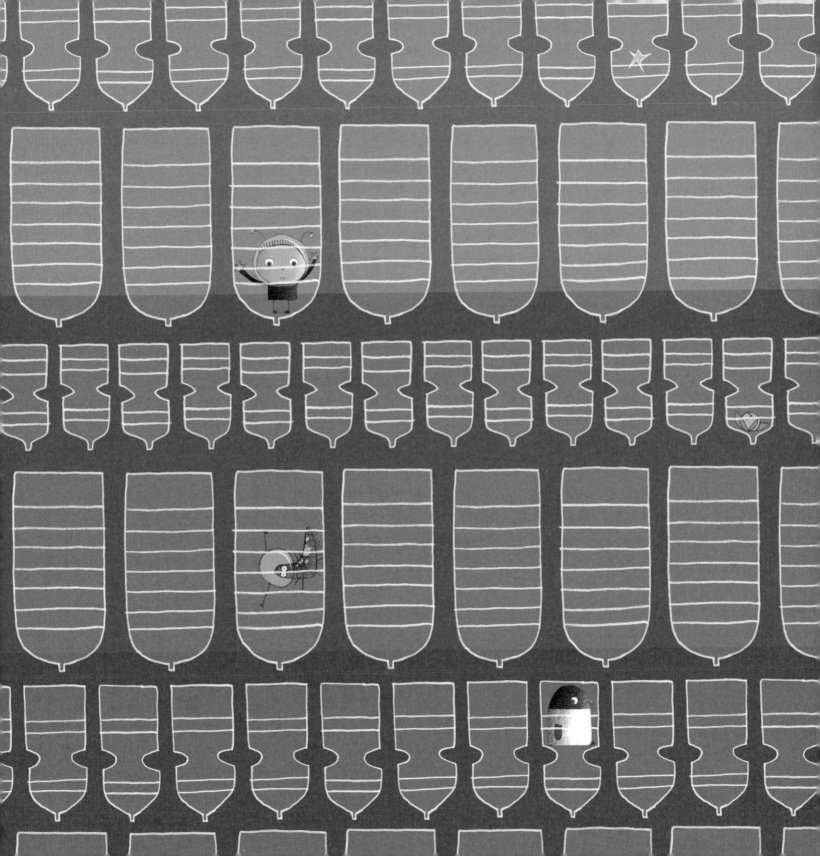

"That's it! There *is* something we can do.
Even if it's something small.

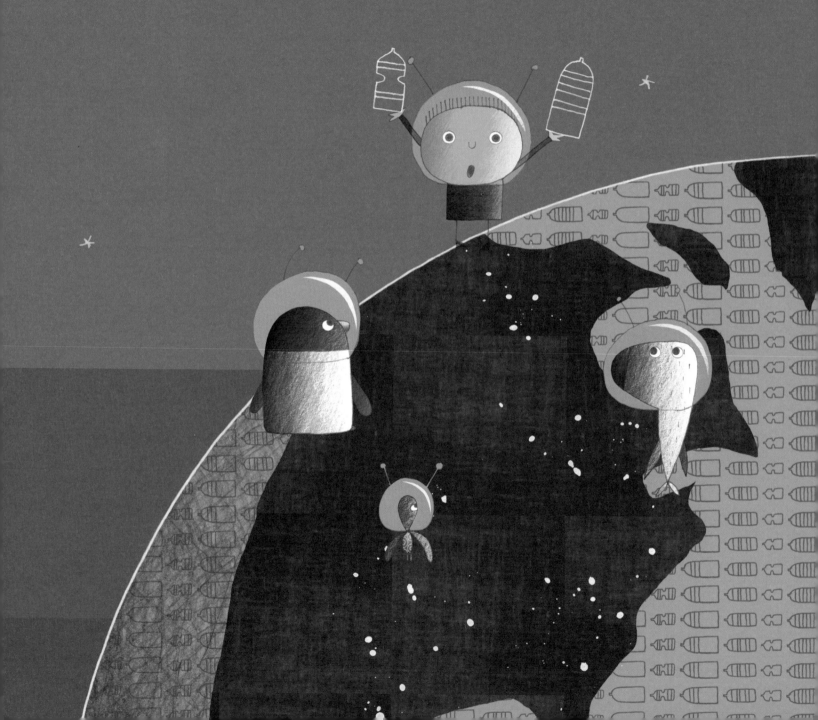

"Because if everyone joins in and helps in a small way ...

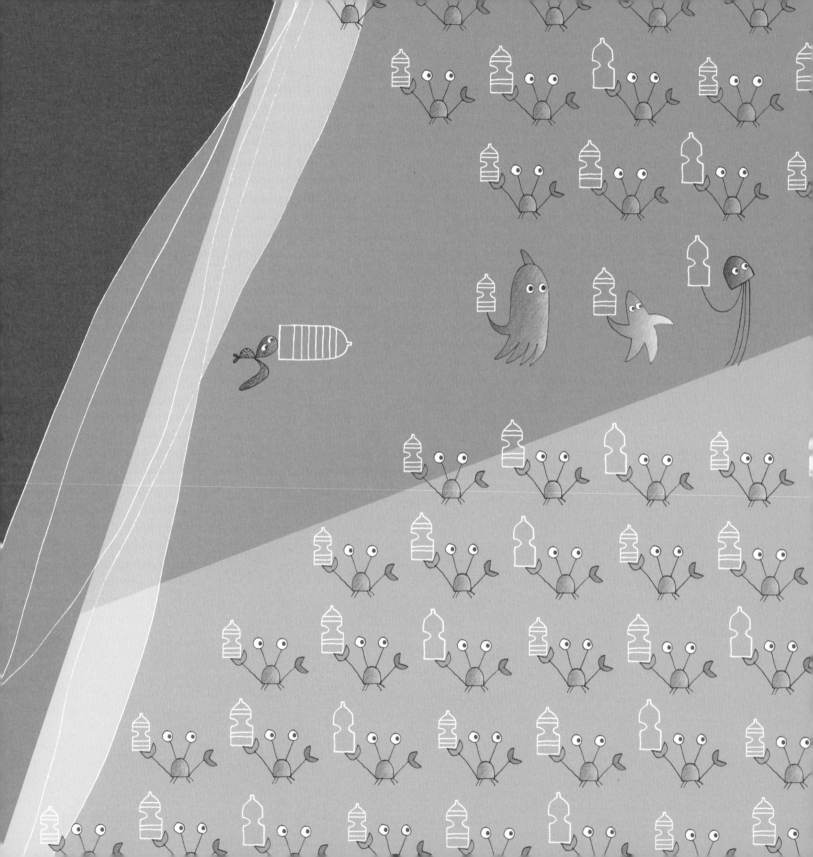

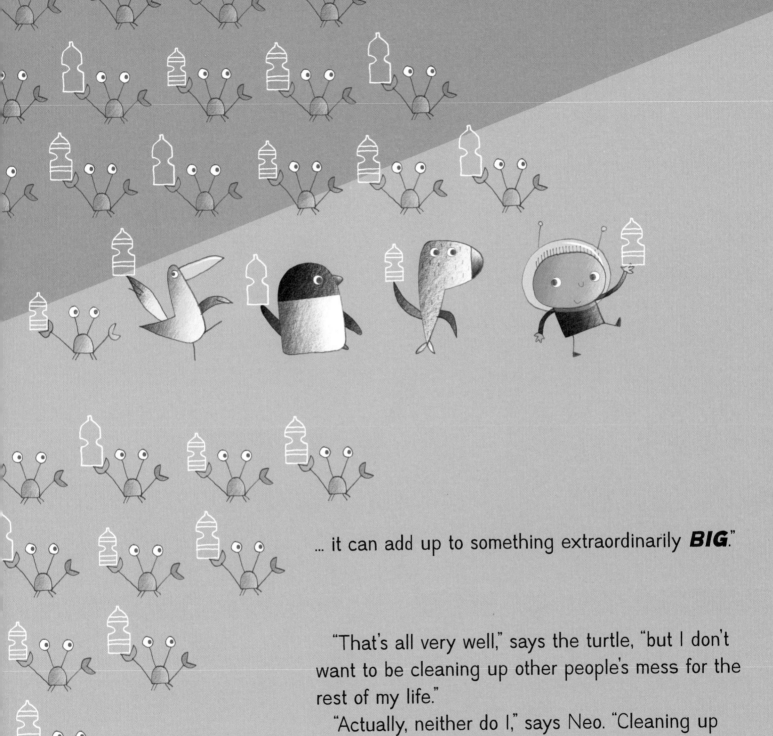

... it can add up to something extraordinarily **BIG**."

"That's all very well," says the turtle, "but I don't want to be cleaning up other people's mess for the rest of my life."

"Actually, neither do I," says Neo. "Cleaning up my own mess is bad enough."

"Then make less mess," says the penguin.

Hmm, thinks Neo. *That is something else I can do.*

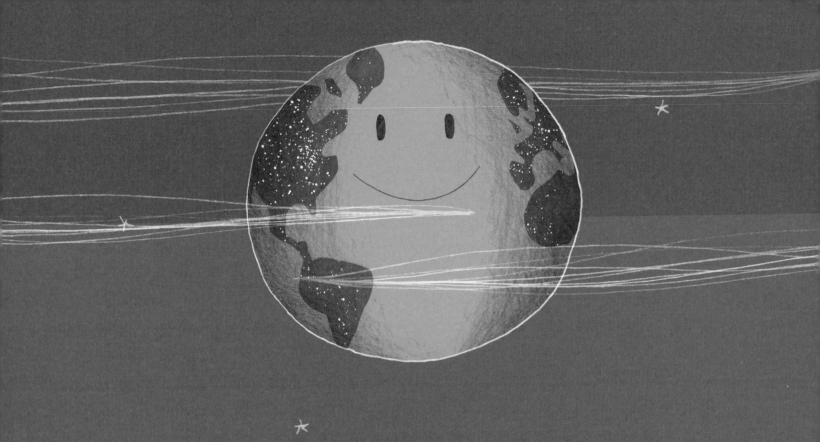

And if everyone around the world also *joins in*
and uses less plastic, planet Earth can be saved
without a single space cabbage being chucked!

When Grandpa arrives home, he can't believe his glasses.
"It's an actual proper miracle! I've never seen your room
looking so clean. And there's an absolute mountain of
recycling outside. What's going on?"

"PLASTIC POLLUTION IS RUINING OUR OCEANS!

THAT'S WHAT'S GOING ON."

Everybody can be an Earth-Bot and help save the planet!

Being an Earth-Bot doesn't mean you have to throw space cabbages to save the planet. You can help by using less plastic.

For every piece of plastic you **REDUCE**, that's one less bit that could end up in the ocean. And one less bit that might end up as Mr. Humpback's breakfast!

You can also **REUSE** non-plastic bags, cups, cutlery and straws. And if everyone had their own refillable water bottle, there wouldn't be a squillion plastic bottles all over the planet.

You can help even more by picking up any litter you find — whether it's in a park, on a beach or in your room. And **RECYCLE** it if you can! That way, it can be made into something else.

It might seem like a lot to do, but it's much easier than chucking cabbages at aliens.

I don't like cabbage anyway.

Speak for yourself.

31901067312795